The Green Frogs

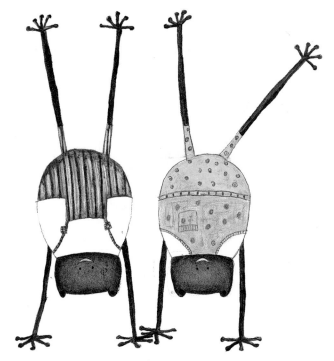

A Korean Folktale Retold by Yumi Heo

Houghton Mifflin Company

Boston

www.houghtonmifflinbooks.com

Manufactured in
the United States of America

Book design by David Saylor
The text of this book is set in
14-point Egmont Medium.
The illustrations are oil paint
and pencil, reproduced in full color.

BVG 10 9 8 7 6 5

*Library of Congress
Cataloging-in-Publication Data*
Heo, Yumi
The green frogs / by Yumi Heo
p. cm.
Summary: A folktale about two green
frogs who always disobey their mother,
explaining why green frogs cry out
whenever it rains.
RNF ISBN 0-395-68378-5 PAP ISBN 0-618-43228-0
[1. Folktale—Korea. 2. Frogs—Folklore]
I. Title   PZ8.1.H403Gr 1996
398.2'095195'04527—dc20[E]
95-19129 CIP AC

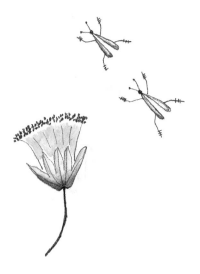

Special thanks to
Norma Jean Sawicki,
Judy Levin,
Morrell Gipson,
David Saylor,
and to Frances Jetter
for all her encouragement.

L̶ong long ago, when tigers still smoked pipes, two green frogs lived with their mother in a lotus pond. The green frogs loved their mother, but they never obeyed her and always did the opposite of what she told them to do.

When spring arrived at the pond, mother frog woke her sons.

"Rise and shine! Spring is here!" she said.

They grumpily pulled their blankets over their heads

and wiggled their toes.

"I know how to get them up," mother frog thought.

She went to the kitchen and
cooked a pot of duckweed soup,
her sons' favorite breakfast.
Sure enough, the green frogs smelled the
delicious soup, and in three jumps they
were in the kitchen.
"Please sit down and eat," she said.
Instead the green frogs giggled
and hopped around with their spoons.

"Well, then, don't eat!" said mother frog.

Right away, the green frogs squatted down

and gobbled up their soup.

It was a messy breakfast.

Mother frog handed each of her sons a wet cloth and a broom.

"Now let's clean up," she said.

But the green frogs tied the wet cloths around their heads

and jumped up and down on the chairs,

leaving footprints all over the kitchen.

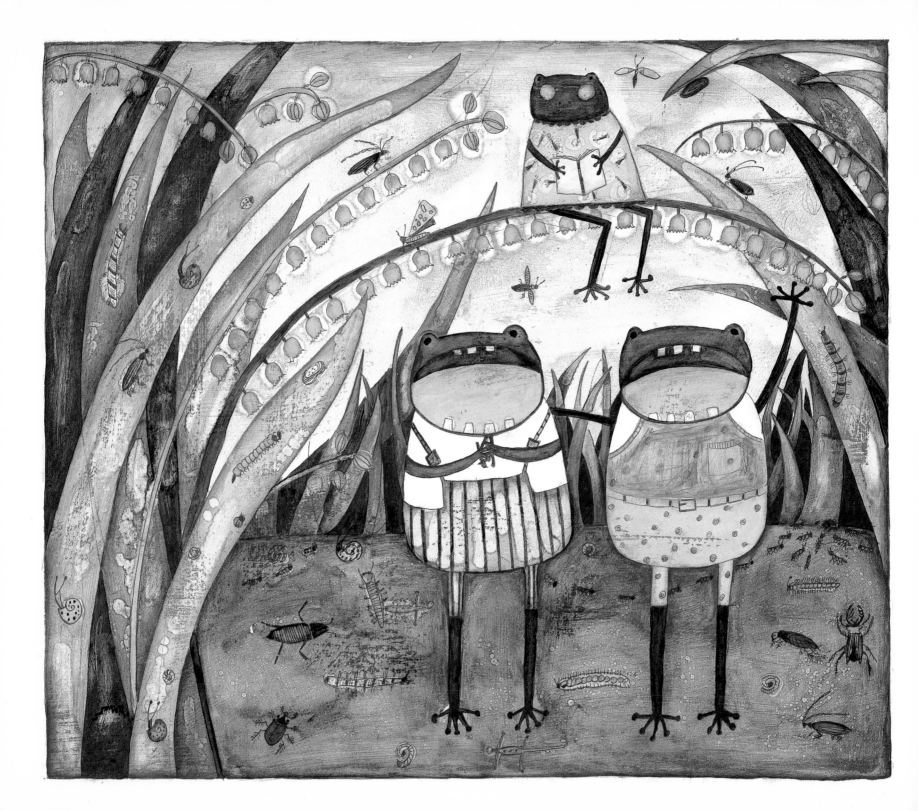

When mother frog finished cleaning up after her sons, she was tired.

All she wanted to do was sit in the tall grass and read her book.

The green frogs were hopping around chasing flies.

"Please be quiet so I can read," she said.

Right away the green frogs began to croak loudly.

"GUL GAE! GUL GAE! GUL GAE!"

"That's not the right way to croak," said mother frog.

"We should have a croaking lesson."

She opened her mouth wide and croaked,

"GAE GUL! GAE GUL! GAE GUL!"

But when it was their turn,

the green frogs again said it backwards.

"GUL GAE! GUL GAE! GUL GAE!"

Mother frog sighed.

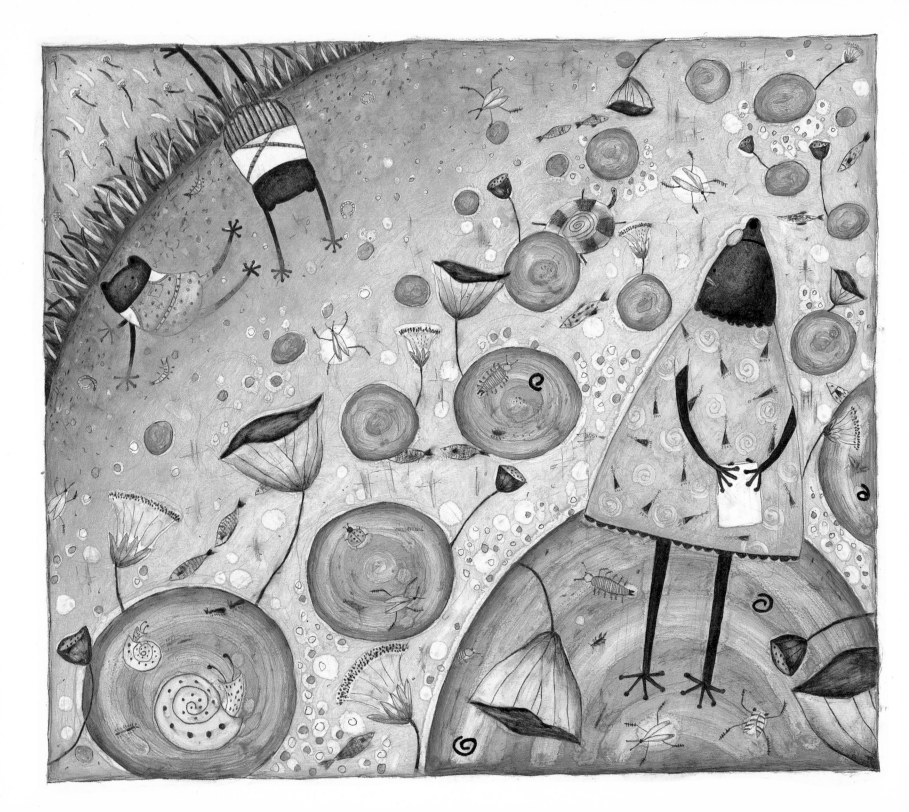

Mother frog picked up her book and hopped back to the house.

"I won't say another word," she thought.

But she couldn't help calling out to her sons,

"Don't get dirty!"

No sooner did the words leave her mouth

than the green frogs jumped into the muddy end of the pond.

They had a great mud fight.

Mother frog shook her head.

So that is the way it went,

through many springs and summers, many falls and winters.

Whatever their mother said, the green frogs would do just the opposite.

When mother frog was very old and sick,

she knew she would soon die.

She wanted to be buried on the sunny side of the hill,

so she told her sons, "Please bury me in the shade by the stream."

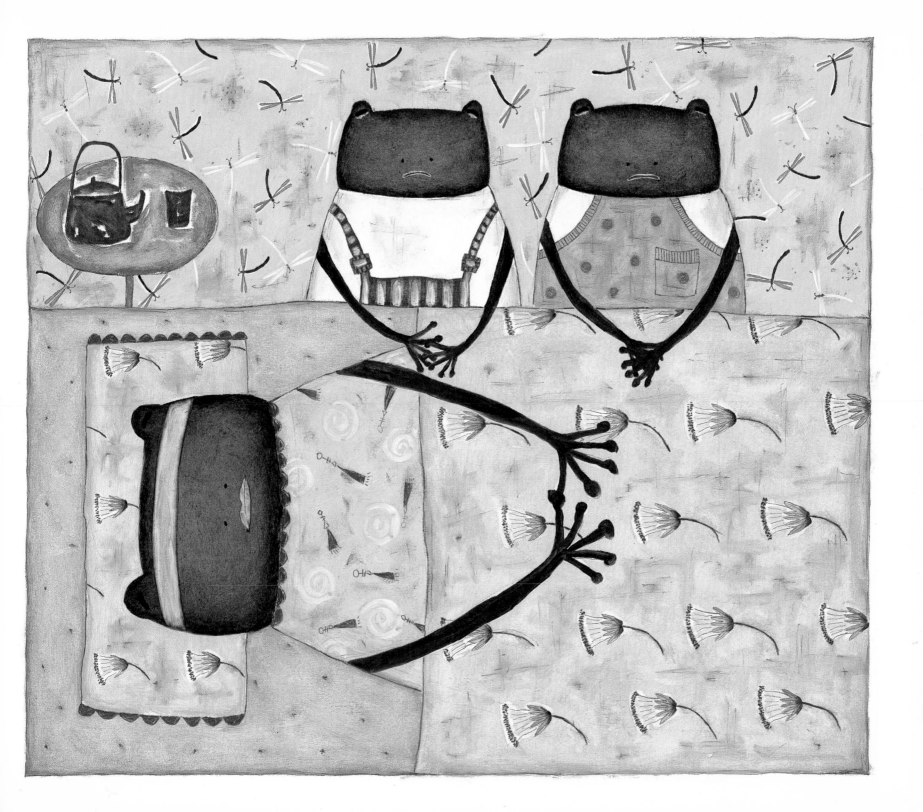

After the mother frog died,

her sons were very sorry they had never listened to her.

They decided to obey her this one last time.

The green frogs buried her by the stream.

That night it began to rain.

It rained for many days and nights,

and the stream overflowed its banks.

The green frogs began to worry

that their mother's grave would wash away.

They went to the stream and cried,

"GAE GUL! GAE GUL! GAE GUL!"

And they begged the stream,

"Please don't wash mother's grave away!"

"Please don't wash mother's grave away!"

And ever since then, whenever it rains,

green frogs sit by streams and cry

"GAE GUL! GAE GUL! GAE GUL!"

And in Korea, children who don't listen to their mother

are called chung-gaeguri or green frogs.